BASEBALL

is for me

BASEBALL
is for me

Lowell A. Dickmeyer

photographs by
Camiel Kannard

 Lerner Publications Company   Minneapolis

The author wishes to thank Camiel Kannard and her son
Chris, the principle character in the book, Dennis and Kevin
O'Shaughnessy, Darlene Davidson, William Darling, Jr.,
Jerry Szostek, Brooks Robinson and the Baltimore Orioles,
and all of the coaches, parents, and players who helped to
make this book possible.

Cover photograph by William Ward

LIBRARY OF CONGRESS CATALOGING IN PUBLICATION DATA

Dickmeyer, Lowell A.
Baseball is for me.

(The Sports for Me Books)
SUMMARY: A young boy relates his experiences as a first-
year Little League player and how he comes to meet Baltimore
Orioles' star Brooks Robinson.

1. Baseball—Juvenile literature. [1. Little League Baseball,
Inc. 2. Baseball] I. Kannard, Camiel. II. Title. III. Series.

GV867.5.D5 1978   796.357'62   77-92299
ISBN 0-8225-1079-0

8883

Manufactured in the United States of America

International Standard Book Number: 0-8225-1079-0
Library of Congress Catalog Card Number: 77-92299

4 5 6 7 8 9 10 90 89 88 87 86 85 84 83 82 81

Hi! I'm Chris, and this is my friend Kevin. We are big baseball fans. This year for the first time we were on a Little League team. On the day before we began practice, Dad took Kevin and me to a real professional baseball game. The Baltimore Orioles were playing the California Angels.

During the game, Dad told Kevin and me to pay close attention to the way each player played his position. Dad said that we could learn a lot about baseball just from watching the players in action.

I especially liked to watch Brooks Robinson play third base. Brooks is my favorite player on the Orioles team. He's retiring this year, so I'm glad I had the chance to see him play.

I was still thinking about Brooks Robinson when I went to Little League practice the next day. I wondered if I would ever play ball as well as Brooks. He made baseball look so easy. I knew that I would have to practice hard to become a good player.

At practice, I met my new teammates and the coach, Mr. Gibson. There were 12 boys on the team. Our team was called the Giants.

Before we started practicing, Coach Gibson called a short meeting to find out how much we knew about baseball.

"Each team in the Little Leagues has nine players and three substitutes," Coach Gibson said as he drew a baseball field on a piece of paper. "Let's name the players as I draw them in."

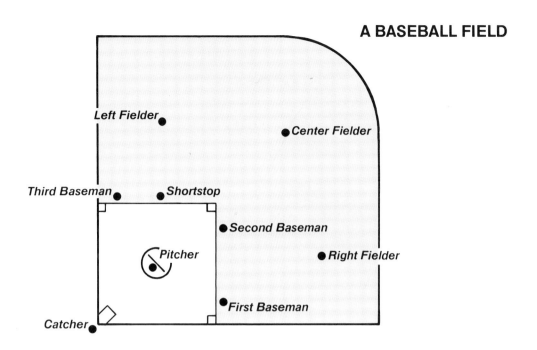

"The six positions within the baseball diamond make up the **infield**," said Coach Gibson. "And the three positions in the grass beyond the diamond are called the **outfield**."

Coach Gibson continued, "In our games, we will play six **innings**. During each inning, both teams take turns batting and playing the field."

"I thought that baseball games were nine innings," said Kevin.

"You are right, Kevin," said Coach Gibson. "The Major League games you see on television are nine innings. High school games are nine innings, too. But Little League rules hold games to six innings. You will be able to play nine-inning games when you are older."

Then the team talked about how baseball is played. Everybody knew a little about the rules of the game. We knew that the team at bat tries to score runs. Runs are scored every time a player moves around all four bases before his team makes three outs.

When the batting team makes three outs, the other team gets a chance to bat and score runs.

"I think that you know enough about the basic rules of baseball to begin practice," said Coach Gibson. "You will learn more about how to play baseball when you practice the different positions. Now run out to the positions you want to play."

To start practice, Coach Gibson hit several balls to each player. The player had to field, or catch, the ball and throw it to the first baseman. The coach hit two kinds of balls to us. His fly balls arched high into the air. We were supposed to catch them before they hit the ground. The **ground balls** bounced before they reached us.

Everyone had butterflies in their stomachs as they waited for their turns to field the ball. When it was my turn, I didn't do very well. I dropped only one fly ball, but every ground ball went past my legs. And my throws went over the first baseman's head.

11

After each boy had his turn catching the ball, Coach Gibson took us to the side of the field. He told us which positions he thought we would play best.

When it was time to talk about where I would play, Coach Gibson said, "Chris, you are having problems catching ground balls. This is an important skill for any third baseman. I think that it would be better if you played in the outfield until you have time to improve. You already have a strong throwing arm. And you are not afraid to catch fly balls. These are two skills that will help you in the outfield."

I still had my heart set on playing third base, but playing outfield was okay, too.

One week later, the Giants met again for practice. I got there early. Some girls were in the park practicing baseball. They were pretty good. In fact, one of the girls said she was on a Little League team, too.

The rest of the Giants soon arrived, and our practice began. The park provided most of the equipment we needed to play baseball: bats, balls, bases, and batting helmets. Each player had to bring his own glove.

During practice, Coach Gibson talked about the different positions on the field. One of the most important players is the pitcher. The pitcher tries to throw the ball within a small area called the **strike zone**. If the batter fails to swing at a pitch in the strike zone, a **strike** is called. A pitch that the batter swings at and misses is also a strike. When a batter gets three strikes, he is out.

Other pitches that do not fall in the strike zone are called **balls**, provided that the batter does not swing at them. When a batter gets four balls, he moves to first base.

The strike zone is an area of space above home plate. The zone falls between a batter's knees and arm pits.

In actual games, an umpire calls balls and strikes. Umpires also call base runners out or safe. Umpires are important because they make sure that everyone plays by the rules.

SAFE

16

OUT

One of the busiest players on the team is the catcher. He stands behind home plate and catches pitches. He also guards the plate when there are runners on base.

To keep from getting hurt, the catcher wears shin guards, a chest pad, and a face mask. The catcher also wears a specially padded glove. The catcher holds the glove out as a target for the pitch.

17

The first, second, and third basemen and the shortstop are the other infield players. They must be especially good at catching ground balls. It is best to move into the path of the ball and bend your knees as you field it. On slow-moving balls, an infielder should run up to meet the ball instead of waiting for it to come to him.

The three outfielders catch long fly balls and any ground balls that go past the infield. Since I was one of the outfielders, I practiced with them. The coach hit many balls to us. We had to keep our eyes on the ball and run to get under it. We used both hands to catch the ball.

I had lots of chances to catch fly balls during our first practice. Before the team left for home, Coach Gibson called a short meeting. He told us who would be starting in our first game on Saturday. Kevin was happy because he was going to be the starting pitcher. I didn't make the first team. Coach Gibson said I would be a substitute outfielder.

19

That afternoon I walked home slowly with Kevin. I was so quiet at home that Mom and Dad asked what was wrong. I told them I wasn't starting in the game on Saturday.

Dad said that he had a good idea. "Why not write to Brooks Robinson? He might give you some good tips on playing baseball."

That sounded like a great idea. After dinner I went up to my room and wrote Brooks a letter.

Dear Mr. Robinson,

This year I am playing for the Giants in our Little League. I did not make the first team because I need to learn more about how to play baseball.

My dad told me to write to you for some help. Would you please send me tips on how to play better? I think baseball is really fun and I would like to play as good as you someday.

Very truly yours,
Chris Kannard

Mom gave me a stamp and an envelope. First thing in the morning, I ran to the mailbox to send off my letter. I couldn't wait to get a letter back from a famous baseball player like Brooks Robinson.

In the meantime, I worked hard to improve my baseball skills. Dad and I went to the park to practice catching, throwing, and hitting.

By Saturday I felt that I was ready for our first game against the Angels. But I spent most of the actual game on the bench. I played in only two innings.

I knew that I would have to keep practicing hard if I were to play more in our next games. Every week we began practice with some stretching exercises. The exercises helped us to warm up. Coach Gibson said that we would have less chance of straining our muscles if we warmed up. We also ran to get in shape. And we did push-ups to make our arms and shoulders stronger.

Each week we also spent some time at batting practice. Each player got six pitches before going back out to the field. Coach Gibson told us to swing level and step into the pitch when we hit.

Our hitting didn't help us much the week we played the Tigers. I watched most of the game from the bench again. It seemed as if the game lasted forever. Kevin had trouble pitching. Several times the ball went over the catcher's head. Each time, the runners would speed ahead to the next base. The Tigers won that game 12-3.

At practice the following week, we worked a lot on catching and throwing. Coach Gibson gave us some good tips on fielding. He said that if you are catching a ball above your waist, you should point your glove up. When catching a ball below your waist, you should point your glove down.

Coach Gibson also told us how to throw using our whole bodies. You should snap the ball and step forward with the opposite foot as you let the ball go. Your arm should continue to follow through after the ball has left your hand.

At first it was hard to remember everything at once. But with practice, we all got better.

Every day I checked the mailbox. I was
sure Brooks Robinson would write. When no
letter came, Mom would say, "Be patient."

But it was hard to be patient. During the games, I was still sitting on the bench. I really wanted to get into the action, especially during exciting games like the one against the Bears. Jeff made a great catch in left field. And Ali had to slide into second base on a **steal**. When you steal a base, you do not wait for the batter to hit the ball before you move ahead to the next base. You try to run to the base when the fielders are not looking. If the fielders are quick, they can throw the ball to the baseman before you get there. Sometimes you have to slide into the base to keep from being tagged out. Stealing is always an exciting play, and I was sure I could do it if I had the chance.

I was pretty discouraged after the game with the Bears. But Mom had a surprise for me when I got home. It was a letter from Brooks Robinson. I opened it as fast as I could.

BALTIMORE ORIOLES

Dear Chris,

Thank you for your nice letter. I am glad that you like baseball and want to learn to play well.

I would very much like to meet with you and give you some tips on how to play good baseball. On July 16 at 7 p.m., the Baltimore Orioles are playing the California Angels. Come early, while we are practicing, and I will spend some time with you. I look forward to seeing you then.

Best always,

Brooks Robinson

Brooks Robinson

P.S. Bring your glove.

I was so excited. I couldn't keep from jumping up and down. I was going to get a chance to play baseball with a real pro! I just knew that Brooks Robinson would be able to help me improve my baseball skills.

I took the letter to school the next day and showed it to my friends. They thought it was neat to get a letter from Brooks Robinson.

The letter really perked my spirits up. During the next practice, Coach Gibson wondered what had happened to me. I was the first player to run out to my position in right field. And when it was my turn to bat, I watched every ball and made some good hits. My second hit went sailing over the shortstop's head for a double!

I still didn't start in the next four games, but I did get to play more innings. The Giants won three games and lost only one. We were tied for first place with the Dodgers. There were only two more weeks until the championship game.

The day I was to meet Brooks Robinson was getting closer and closer, too. Finally the day came.

On the way to the stadium, I was a little nervous. Dad reminded me that Brooks was a person like everyone else. "He likes kids and will enjoy helping you," Dad said.

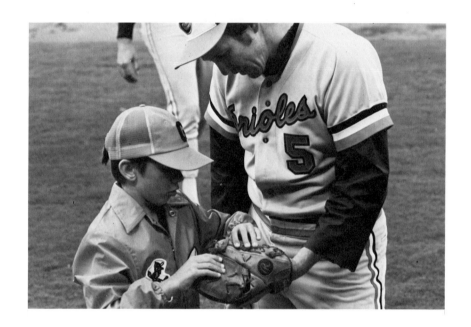

Sure enough, Brooks was down by the dugout waiting for us. He asked me what position I played. I told him right field. Brooks laughed and said, "That's where I started playing, too."

Brooks and I got our gloves and started playing ball right there on that big baseball field. It was such a big stadium. I felt like I was playing Big League baseball before thousands of people.

I listened very carefully when Brooks showed me how to catch the ball. Then we went into the team dugout to talk.

Brooks and I had only a little time to talk before the game. He told me how important it was to always try hard at any position I was playing.

I told Brooks about the Giants and my first season on the team. I also told him about the championship game that was coming up.

My visit with Brooks was soon over. The last thing he said to me was, "Good luck in the championship game!"

After meeting Brooks Robinson, I could hardly wait to play baseball again. Before I knew it, the championship game was here.

On the morning of the game, I grabbed my glove and ran all the way to the game. My eyes almost popped out of my head when I saw Coach Gibson pointing at me. "Chris," he said, "you're starting in right field today." My heart was pounding as I quickly ran to my position.

Not much happened in the first two innings. Both pitchers were firing the ball hard and right over the plate. With a big swoosh, Steve struck out, making the second out for our team. I stepped in to bat.

The infielders were playing deep, so Coach Gibson signaled me to **bunt**. A bunt is a soft hit. The batter does not swing the bat on a bunt. He just brings the bat up to meet the ball. The first pitch came in, and I bunted it down the first baseline. The pitcher rushed to field the ball. But he wasn't fast enough. I beat his throw to first base.

Peter was the next batter. He hit the ball all the way to the outfield fence. I scored. Then the Dodgers shortstop made an error, or mistake. He wasn't looking when the outfielder threw the ball back into the infield. The ball went past the diamond. Peter rounded third base and scored, too. Now the score was the Giants 2 and the Dodgers 1.

The score was still the same in the last inning when the Dodgers came to bat. But they had a runner on second base and one out still to go.

All of a sudden, the batter hit a hard ground ball to right field. I rushed to it, snagged the ball in my glove, and fired it to the catcher. The ball came just in time to get the Dodger sliding home. He was out!

The crowd went wild. The Giants were the champions! I was so glad that I helped the team with a big play. It was an exciting way to end the season.

Kevin stayed at my house that night. We talked for hours about that final game. Before going to sleep, I took one last look at our championship trophy. Playing right field wasn't so bad after all!

Words about BASEBALL

BALL: A pitch that is outside the strike zone and that the batter fails to swing at

BUNT: A pitch that is met and tapped by the bat. The batter does not make a full swing with the bat.

CHARGE: To run up to a ball to field it rather than wait for the ball to come to you

DOUBLE HEADER: Two baseball games played one right after the other

DOUBLE PLAY: A play in which two runners are tagged out or forced out on the same batted ball

ERROR: A mistake by a player fielding the ball, such as a dropped ball or an overthrow

FOUL BALL: A batted ball that lands to the left or to the right of the playing area of the baseball field

HIT: A ball that lands in the playing area of the baseball field and that advances the batter safely to at least one base

INFIELD: That part of the playing area right around the baseball diamond. The catcher, pitcher, first baseman, second baseman, shortstop, and third baseman play in the infield.

INNING: A part of a baseball game in which both teams have a chance to bat and make three outs apiece

OUTFIELD: That part of the playing area in the field beyond the baseball diamond. The right fielder, center fielder, and left fielder play in the outfield.

STRIKE: A pitch that
    a) the batter swings at and misses
    b) is in the strike zone but that the batter fails to swing at
    c) is fouled by a batter who has less than two strikes

STRIKE ZONE: The area of space above home plate that is between the batter's arm pits and knees

TAG: The fielder's act of touching a runner with the ball or with his glove holding the ball

ABOUT THE AUTHOR

LOWELL A. DICKMEYER is active in athletics as a participant, instructor, and writer. He is particularly interested in youth sport programs, and each summer he organizes sports camps for hundreds of youngsters. Mr. Dickmeyer has been a college physical education instructor and an elementary school principal in southern California.

ABOUT THE PHOTOGRAPHER

CAMIEL KANNARD is active in the fields of fine arts and photography. She has taught painting in secondary schools and more recently has become a student of photography. Ms. Kannard is a member of the Thousand Oaks (California) Arts Council and a past member of the Greenwich Art Society, New York City.